The Big Blue Eggventure:
The Hatching of Baby Jay

Story by Deeann Downs and Jennifer Embrey Orth
Pictures by Katherine Trueman-Gardner

Printed in the United States of America by Anchor Press, Inc.

ISBN 0-9658392-0-6

Library of Congress 97-091921

In memory of my father, "The Old Wildcat."
To Tim and Aleksander, my two favorite Jayhawks.
D.S.D.

To my parents, Orville and Judy,
for your lifelong love, prayers, and encouragement.
To my husband, Fabian, for your love and belief in this project.
To my children, Rebekah and Cameron, with love.
"All things are possible to him who believes." Mark 9:23
J.E.O.

For Mark. My life, my love, my friend. Your support on this book
and in every endeavor in my life means more to me than words can say.
K.T.G.

On the day of the
Kansas and Kansas State
football game, Willie
Wildcat was making
mischief of one kind and
another around
Mount Oread.

He put *bubble bath* in the Chi Omega Fountain,

he wrote, "Go Wildcats!" in front of Strong Hall with purple chalk, and he was just about to take the KU flag from the top of Fraser Hall when he saw the most beautiful blue egg in all of Kansas. Willie stopped and gazed at the big, blue egg tucked safely away in a golden nest made of the finest Kansas wheat.

He gently rubbed
the blue egg
with his paw,
leaving a purple
paw print on
the shiny shell.

The wildcat reached down
and picked up the blue egg.
Just as he hugged the
beautiful egg in his arms,
it began to rumble.
Surprised, the clumsy
wildcat fumbled the egg.

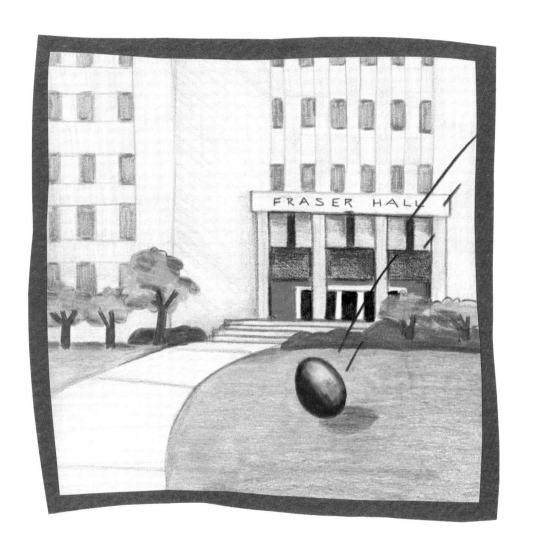

The old wildcat watched nervously as the big, blue egg went spiraling through the air like a football and made a wobbly landing in front of Fraser Hall.

The big, blue egg kept wobbling and wobbling until it began to roll.
It rolled over the lawn of Watson Library,

across Wescoe Beach,

and down Jayhawk Boulevard toward the Chi Omega Fountain foaming with *bubbles*.

When the big, blue egg reached the fountain, it began to spin like a top on the slippery soap the wildcat had carelessly left behind.

As the spinning slowed,
the egg began to rock
back and forth on
the sudsy sidewalk.
At last the egg tumbled
end over end down the
hill toward Potter Lake,
picking up speed as
it came closer to
the murky water.

The big, blue egg rolled and rolled until it skipped, **splish splash splish splash,** across Potter Lake like a stone flicked from a young boy's hand.

After the last skip,
the egg ricocheted off
the bridge and went
flying through the air
and landed with a
thump-bump-bump
at the base of
Memorial Campanile.

From a distance, the roar of enthusiastic fans cheering on the Jayhawk football team could be heard. The thundering noise caused the big, blue egg to teeter back and forth until the egg began to roll down the hill toward the cheering crowd at Memorial Stadium.

The egg tumbled down the sidewalk and through the stadium gates and gradually rolled to a stop in the middle of the football field.

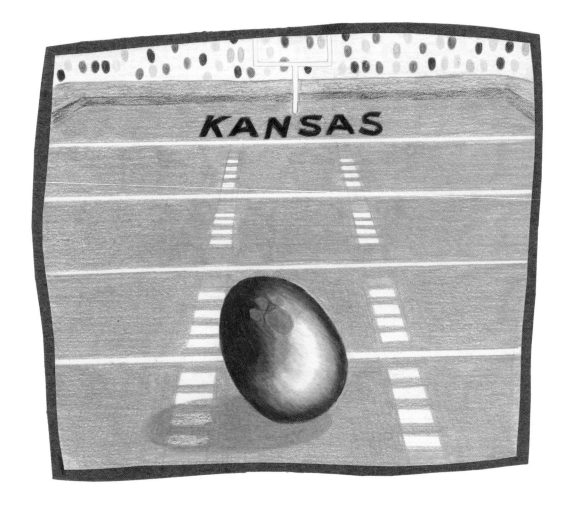

Jay Jayhawk recognized the big, blue egg, scarred with a purple paw print, and suspected Willie Wildcat had been up to no good. Looking around, Jay spotted the old wildcat stumbling down the hill toward Memorial Stadium.

The fans, astonished at
the arrival of the big, blue
egg, stared in silent awe
at the beautiful egg
resting in the center
of the grassy field.
Jay Jayhawk carefully
rubbed off the purple
paw print that tarnished
the blue shell.

Then, the shiny, blue shell began to crack.

Peck, peck, peck!
Craaack!

Peck, peck, peck!
Craaack!

POP!

Out from the big, blue egg hatched the most beautiful bird in all of Kansas, a baby Jayhawk.

The fans whistled
and cheered the
arrival of the
beautiful bird and
began to chant,

"*Baby Jay!*
Baby Jay!
Baby Jay!"

Jay Jayhawk proudly marched Baby Jay around the field,
as the band played "I'm a Jayhawk."

While Jay Jayhawk and Baby Jay waved to the cheering fans, the old wildcat clung tightly to the goal post in the Kansas end zone.

Willie Wildcat knew
he had *been* defeated.
With the *sound* of the
cheering fans ringing
in his ears, he scrambled
back up the hill to return
to his own school, still
frightened to this day
by the mighty Jayhawks.

The Birth of Baby Jayhawk

Homecoming 1971 marked the birth of the baby Jayhawk. During the halftime show of the Kansas and Kansas State football game, a large, blue egg was pulled toward the center of the field. The Jayhawk proudly watched as the baby Jayhawk hatched from the blue egg. Baby Jay arrived just in time to see the Jayhawks beat the Wildcats 39-13.

About the Authors and Illustrator

Deeann Downs received a Bachelor of Science degree in Education from the University of Kansas and a Masters Degree in Elementary Education from Arizona State University. After teaching elementary school for six years, she is now a full-time mom. She and her husband, Tim, have one son, Aleksander, and live in Arizona. This is her first children's book.

Jennifer Embrey Orth graduated from the University of Kansas with a Bachelor of Science degree in Elementary/Middle Education. She taught middle school English and mathematics for three years before becoming a full-time mom. She and her husband, Fabian, live in Ohio with their two children, Rebekah and Cameron. This is her first children's book.

Katherine Trueman-Gardner attended KU for four and a half years as an illustration major before making the switch to education. She received a Bachelor of Science degree in Art Education from Emporia State University and a Masters Degree in Education from MidAmerica Nazarene College. She is currently a junior high art teacher. She and her husband, Mark, live in Kansas with their dog, Tucker. This is the first children's book she has illustrated.

Distributed by:
The KU Bookstores
Jayhawk Boulevard
The University of Kansas
Lawrence, KS 66045-1963
(785)-864-4640

To order additional copies call:
1-800-4KU-1111
Fax: (785)-864-5264
e-mail: jayhawks@ukans.edu
web site: www.jayhawks.com